BITING FOR BLOOD

CHOOSE YOUR OWN

NIGHTMARE... #7

BITING FOR BLOOD
BY EDWARD PACKARD

ILLUSTRATED BY BILL SCHMIDT

BANTAM BOOKS
NEW YORK · TORONTO · LONDON · SYDNEY · AUCKLAND

RL 4, age 008–012

BITING FOR BLOOD
A Bantam Book/February 1996

ISBN 0-553-48359-5

Published simultaneously in the United States and Canada

PRINTED IN THE UNITED STATES OF AMERICA

OPM   0   9   8   7   6   5   4   3   2   1

BITING FOR BLOOD

WARNING!

You have probably read books where scary things happen to people. Well, in *Choose Your Own Nightmare*, you're right in the middle of the action. The scary things are happening to you!

When bloodless bodies start turning up around town, there's only one explanation: A vampire is on the loose!

Fortunately, while you're reading along, you'll have chances to decide what to do. Whenever you make a decision, turn to the page shown. The thrills and chills that happen to you next will depend on your choices.

Be sure to choose carefully. A vampire may be breathing down your neck.

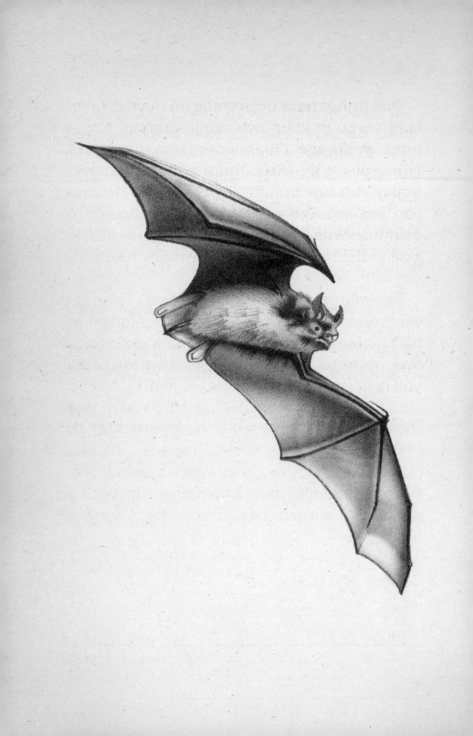

1

Odd things have been going on in your town lately, even in your own neighborhood. About three weeks ago a man moved into the big old house down the street from your house. Yesterday you saw him for the first time. The sun had just set, and you were coming home on your bike when you saw him walk through the gate in the brick wall that surrounds his property.

The man was wearing black pants, a white shirt, and a dark red cape that hung loose on his shoulders. His black hair was slicked back over his head. He reminded you of a magician you once saw. But there was something creepy about him—he looked like no one you'd ever seen.

His face was pale, yet his lips were a shiny bright red. He looked at you for an instant, his eyes glowing like those of a jungle cat. With a shiver, you turned away and pedaled toward home.

Turn to page 2.

You and your friends, Brian and Jenny Conrad, are sitting in Sam's Soda Shop. Brian and Jenny are twins who live a couple of blocks from your house. They listen intently while you tell them about the strange-looking man.

"He might be a vampire," Brian says.

"Most people think vampires don't really exist," Jenny says. "But I think they do. There could be one on the loose in this town! On the radio this morning they said another person is missing."

"That makes three in the past month," Brian says. "And did you hear about the dead deer they found in the woods behind the library? All its blood was drained out." Then his expression changes. He's looking at a newspaper on the table next to you. A headline halfway down the page reads:

POLICE CHIEF DENIES VAMPIRE
MAY HAVE CAUSED RECENT CRIMES

Turn to page 4.

4

"Can we believe him?" you ask.

"He probably doesn't want people to panic," Brian says.

"What other explanation could there be for that deer?" Jenny asks. She looks at you. "Are you thinking what I'm thinking?"

You nod. "The man I was talking about."

"Did you find out anything about him?" asks Brian.

"I asked my mom," you say. "She said she heard that a man named Eliot Sanger had bought that house, but no one she talked to had seen him."

"Maybe we ought to call Maria Murton," Jenny says. "She's a friend of our mom's who's a newspaper reporter. She may be looking into this."

Brian tilts back his glass to get an ice cube out of the bottom. "Maybe we should investigate Sanger ourselves," he says. "We could go up to the front door and say we're looking for a job raking leaves or something."

"We might end up having to rake leaves," Jenny says.

Go on to the next page.

"We might end up being victims of a vampire," you say.

"Maybe we should check out the house from the outside first," Brian says.

Jenny has a skeptical look on her face. "What could we tell from looking at the house?"

"He's got to come out to get groceries and stuff," you say.

Jenny shrugs. "Maybe he gets everything delivered."

"He doesn't need groceries," Brian says. "He just drinks blood. *Yaaaahhhheee!*" He makes a low, shrieking noise.

"I'm going to go home and call Maria Murton," Jenny says. "Why don't you come along?"

Turn to page 6.

"Or you can come with me," Brian says. "I'm going to check out Sanger's house right now."

You think for a moment about which plan sounds better. You're also thinking it might be a good idea to read up on vampires in the library. That way you might get a better idea of how to recognize them.

If you decide to go to the library and read up on vampires, turn to page 14.

If you decide to go back with Jenny to her house, turn to page 27.

If you decide to go with Brian to check out Sanger's house, turn to page 37.

Shielding your eyes, you bulldoze your way through the underbrush. Twigs and thorns scratch your face as you go by. You know better than to cry out, but when you reach up with your hand, you feel drops of blood on your face.

You don't mind getting cut, but what if the vampire can smell your blood?

You can't worry about it—you've got to keep moving. You work your way out of the heavy brush and pick up speed, moving deeper into the woods.

You hear a man's voice coming from Brian and Jenny's house. It sounds like the vampire, angry that no one is there. By now you don't care which way you're going or whether you find your friends—you just want to get as far away as possible!

Soon you're so deep in the woods you can't see any light from the Conrad house. At last, you feel safe. If the vampire were able to track you down, he probably would have gotten you by now.

Turn to page 12.

8

"Just a moment," he says. "Wouldn't you like to look inside the coffin? I'll lift up the lid."

"No, thanks." You turn to leave, but a powerful sleepy feeling is taking hold of you. You're afraid you're going to fall over. You slump into a chair, your eyes closing heavily. You open them for a second and see Mr. Gravesend standing over you. A moment later you slump down, unconscious.

Turn to page 56.

Deciding to wait, you climb up and sit on the brick wall, facing the house with your legs dangling down.

Time passes. Maria doesn't come out. You're beginning to worry about her. It's hard to know what to do.

You wait patiently until the sun slips behind the trees. By now you're more worried than ever. The sun will be setting in a few minutes. If Sanger *is* a vampire, he will be getting out of his coffin at sunset. Maria will be in terrible danger. Maybe you should try to warn her. On the other hand, you don't want to open the door to that house when a vampire is waking up! Maybe you should call the police.

If you decide to call the police, turn to page 33.

If you decide to open the door to the house and see if you can warn Maria, turn to page 59.

10

"Mr. Gravesend came home and found you here. He called me. I already called all of your friends—I was worried sick. No one knew where you were.

"Mr. Gravesend is a carpenter who makes coffins for a living," your mom continues. "It was quite a shock for him to come home and find someone lying in one of them."

Mr. Gravesend smiles at you. "What were you thinking, child? Coming into someone's home like that and lying in a coffin!"

You glare at him. He drugged you with the cookies and put you in a coffin. He's mixed up with the vampire and he's lying to protect the monster and himself! He knows it, and you know it. The question is, how are you going to convince anyone else?

The End

You go up to the front door of the house, cautiously open it, and look inside. From this angle you can see into an entrance hall. A mirror hangs on the wall, and a broad, curving staircase leads up to the second floor.

To your left is a living room. Heavy drapes on the windows block out nearly all outside light. Otherwise, the room is lit by a single dim lamp.

To your right is a dining room with a long, narrow table which has only two chairs, one at each end.

You hear a noise from somewhere in the house. You tiptoe through the dining room and carefully open the door at the far end. It leads to a large pantry. The door at the far end of the pantry is open. You guess it leads to the kitchen.

At that moment an enormous brown dog charges into the room. It stops short a few feet away from you. You're startled, but then you relax a little as you realize it's not going to attack you.

The dog doesn't growl or bark. It just stands there, glaring at you.

Turn to page 50.

12

You know the woods doesn't stretch very far. If you just keep going you'll come out on your own street. Your parents will sure be surprised to have you come home at this hour!

It's almost impossible to walk in a straight line through the woods, especially on a dark night. But soon you see a light ahead.

By now it's pretty late. Most houses are dark, so you can't tell which one you're headed for. You just keep going.

A large house with only one dim light showing looms up in the darkness. A few moments later, as you come out of the woods, the ground seems to drop out from under you—you have to jump to keep from stumbling. Fortunately, you land on your feet. Turning around, you see that you've walked over a two-foot-high rock ledge. There's a tiny cave set in it.

You continue on, moving through the tall, unmowed grass toward the big house. You can cut across the yard and reach the street in no time.

Turn to page 39.

"You killed him," he says in a low, steady voice. "You killed my stepson Eliot."

"I didn't mean to," you say. "Besides, if he was a vampire . . ."

Before you can finish your sentence, Mr. Gravesend swings at you with his cane. He looks old and feeble, but he moves fast. You barely manage to duck around him. As you pass the coffin, the shriveled, smoking hand of the dead vampire brushes against you. You feel its long fingernails passing across your arm, drawing blood.

Mr. Gravesend swings at you again. His cane barely misses your back as you twist away. Screaming, you race outside, never looking back as you run toward home.

When you get to your house, you examine the scratches on your arm where the vampire's fingernails brushed you. Drops of blood are still oozing from the wounds. You wash your arm with soap and water and splash on some hydrogen peroxide. The bleeding soon stops. But the scratches never heal.

The End

14

At the library you ask where to find books about vampires. Ms. Hallowell, the librarian, shows you one titled *History of the Vampires*. The only trouble is that it's about seven hundred pages long.

"I've actually done a study of vampires," she tells you. "What in particular do you want to know?"

"Just how to recognize them, and what they do," you say.

"Well," she says, "according to legend, vampires live on the blood of animals and people. They don't have much trouble catching their victims because they have superhuman strength. Unless they are caught out while the sun is up, they can live forever!

"Fortunately, vampires have some weaknesses. They can't stand daylight—they have to sleep in their coffins all day long and only come out after sunset. Most experts say that you can scare them away with garlic. But there are cases of vampires who weren't stopped by this at all."

Turn to page 36.

"Let's try the garlic," you say.

More pounding sounds at the front door.

"C'mon!" Jenny yells. You and Brian race after her to the kitchen. You watch as she separates garlic cloves. She starts trying to peel them and cut them up.

"That's too slow!" Brian snaps. He pulls a hammer out of a drawer, shoves Jenny aside, and pounds on the cloves. You smell the strong odor of garlic as the juice runs out.

The pounding on the front door continues. The vampire is really mad. You all smear garlic on your faces and necks. It really smells, but if that's what it takes, you're not going to complain.

Now the *back* door is rattling!

"That's not a strong door!" Brian cries.

"That's all right—we're ready!" Jenny says in a brave voice. But you have a feeling she's just as scared as you are. Suddenly the door gives way! A cold wind sweeps into the room.

Turn to page 70.

The three of you duck behind the bushes. Sanger reaches the wall and again vaults over it with ease. Then he turns and walks down the street in the opposite direction.

"Maybe we should follow him," Brian says.

"Too dangerous. And besides, it's almost dark," Jenny says.

Brian nods. "See you tomorrow," he says, nudging you in the arm.

"You'd better go home, too," Jenny tells you. "It's not safe."

But you stay there after they've left, still curious to see where the man is going.

If you decide to follow him,
turn to page 24.

If you decide just to come back and watch for him
the following night, turn to page 57.

"I'm Detective Paterno," he says. "We would have been here sooner but we were looking for clues to help crack this case."

"What case?" you ask. "What happened?"

"There may have been some foul play at the Sanger house after all. That reporter—Maria Murton—is missing," Detective Paterno tells you.

"We got a search warrant to go through the house," Officer Swartz adds. "We didn't find Ms. Murton, or Mr. Sanger. But we did find something behind a false wall in the master bedroom."

"What?" you ask eagerly.

Turn to page 84.

18

You start back toward the front door. The dog stands up, growling.

"It's okay, boy. I'm leaving, just like you want me to," you say soothingly.

The dog bares its teeth. It crouches, ready to spring. But you keep moving and talking. By now you're a little past it. Another couple of steps, and you'll be able to get through the door and slam it behind you.

A shrill whistle sounds from somewhere in the house. The dog starts leaping in the air, wagging its tail.

What's going on? You don't take time to guess. You're through the door in a flash, slamming it behind you. The dog didn't even follow you!

Now you're in the dining room. You're about to make a run for the front door when you see the mirror in the hallway ahead. Reflected in it is a tall man with dark hair, pale skin, and scarlet lips. Sanger!

"Ahhh!" you scream, dashing back into the pantry. Fortunately, the dog is gone. You race through to the kitchen, hoping it has a back door.

Turn to page 73.

You know you shouldn't go into a stranger's house, but the little old man seems harmless—even friendly. And he's piqued your curiosity with his knowledge of vampires.

"All right," you say. "I accept." The man gives you a smile. He motions for you to follow him as he limps toward his own door.

Mr. Gravesend's home is completely different from the gloomy mansion across the street. It's a freshly painted white clapboard house with nice trees and a neat, well-trimmed lawn. He shows you into his sunny kitchen and invites you to sit at a table covered with a red checkerboard cloth. He puts out some cookies and cider and sits down across from you.

"Thanks," you say.

"I think you'll like them," he says. He watches, hawklike, while you cautiously nibble on a cookie. It's okay, but you've tasted better.

"What would you like to know about vampires?" he asks.

"Whatever you know," you say.

Turn to page 76.

"Him or her. Some vampires are female," Ms. Hallowell corrects you. "As to how to recognize them, well, vampires are very strong. Some people say they have straight, oily black hair, but that may not always be the case. Their faces are usually very pale, their lips red, and if they open their mouths, you can see their fangs. They look like the fangs of a wolf. Otherwise, the only way to be sure someone is a vampire is by their eyes. Their eyes may be brown, gray, or green, but they are always very bright, almost as if a fire were lighting them from the inside." Ms. Hallowell looks at you. "Are you feeling all right? You don't look well."

"I'm okay," you say. "I was just thinking about a man I saw—he looked a lot like what you described."

Turn to page 60.

You make it to the kitchen door and open it just enough to slide through. You slam the door shut behind you, right on the dog's nose! It backs up with a yelp, barks loudly, and hurls itself against the door. You hope the vampire is still sleeping. If he isn't, he'll find you in no time!

You listen to the dog growling behind the door. There's no doubt it would sink its teeth into you if it could. You turn around, looking for an escape route. Again the dog lunges against the door. You lean hard against it to keep it shut. But slowly it opens, wider, wider . . .

A figure appears in the doorway. Eliot Sanger, risen from his coffin! He lunges at you with superhuman speed. A second later you feel his long, curving fangs piercing your neck.

The End

22

You close your eyes and toss and turn for what seems like hours. Finally you doze off. Sometime later you wake with a start. A hand is resting on your shoulder. Moonlight streams through the window, shining on a pale figure standing over your bed. It's Maria!

But not the Maria you met earlier! She seems bigger, stronger. Her hair hangs limply around her face, which is the color of paste.

Her eyes burn into you. She smiles. Her lips part, and you see her sharp, curved fangs, coming closer, closer . . .

The End

24

You follow Sanger as he strides down the street. You get the feeling he's not just out for a walk—he is headed someplace in particular.

Coming toward you is a woman walking a large, shaggy dog. Sanger gets closer to them. The dog starts growling and pulling on his leash.

The woman pulls him along. "Dusty! What's gotten into you?"

She finally gets her dog under control. The man walks on, ignoring them.

You duck into the shadows while the woman and her dog pass by. When you next look for Sanger, you don't see him, which is surprising because the street is quite straight and well lit.

You want to keep following him, but you're afraid he might ambush you as you go by. You turn to start toward home . . . and bump right into him! He looms over you, his face deathly pale.

Turn to page 85.

Officer Swartz drives you to the Sanger house. You follow a few steps behind as he walks up to the front door. By now the sun has set, though there's still quite a bit of light in the sky.

Officer Swartz knocks on the door. There's no answer. He knocks again, rapping loudly with his nightstick.

Still no answer. It may be too late to save Maria!

He tries the door. "It's locked," he says. "Well, that's about all I can do."

"Aren't you going to break the door open?"

He takes your elbow, guiding you back toward his patrol car. "That would be breaking the law," he tells you. "I have no evidence a crime has been committed. I don't have a search warrant, and a judge wouldn't give me one."

Turn to page 49.

26

Still he keeps coming. Something about the way he walks and talks begins to hypnotize you.

"I will let you go," he says softly. "But you must promise never to tell that you saw me. I make a promise, and you make a promise."

There is no hope of your making it to the street, and running back into the woods looks pretty hopeless, too. You have only one other choice—to hide in the little cave you just passed. It's too small for the vampire to fit in. You could wait there until dawn if necessary. He couldn't get you. At least you don't think so.

He takes another slow step toward you. "Do you promise?" he repeats.

If he gets any closer, he'll be able to catch you before you make it to the cave!

If you run to the cave,
turn to page 79.

If you stay where you are and promise not to tell
about meeting him, turn to page 40.

You and Jenny bike over to her house, but you have no luck reaching Maria Murton on the phone.

"Oh, well. Let's see if there's anything about the vampire on the evening news," Jenny says. "Why don't you stay for dinner? My parents are going out. We'll have the whole place to ourselves."

"I don't think my mom will let me walk home after dark," you say. "Not with a vampire around, anyway."

"Stay overnight. We have a guest room, you know," Jenny says.

You stop by your house, get the okay from your mom, and bike over to the twins' house. By then Brian has returned, but he has nothing to report.

Mrs. Conrad puts out a macaroni and cheese casserole and tells you all to heat it up in the microwave when you want to have dinner. "Dad and I will be back around eight-thirty," she tells the twins.

Turn to page 58.

You take no chances with the old man and run for home. Once you're safely inside, you try to make sense of what's happened.

Why did Gravesend accuse you of spying? What difference would it make to him if you were standing there? You weren't even that close to his property!

Your parents get home soon afterward. You tell them the whole story. They call the police, and soon afterward a detective and two officers stop by your house.

The detective listens as you repeat what you told your parents. When you finish, he says, "We've been looking for a break in the vampire case. This could be it!"

"What happens next?" you ask.

"We can't tell you," the detective says, "but there's no need to worry. We're going to act very soon."

Turn to page 35.

By now the room is getting darker. You glance at your watch. The sun will be setting soon—it may already have set! Once the vampire gets out of his coffin, it won't take him long to find you. You've got to make a break for it soon!

The dog is lying down again, its eyes half closed. This is your chance to make it into the kitchen. But what you really want to do is get back to the front door, and you'd have to walk right by the dog to do that. Maybe you could get by it if you spoke to it in a soothing voice.

Gong . . . Gong . . . Gong . . . Gong . . . Gong . . . Gong. The hall clock is striking six. You don't dare wait any longer.

If you try to get past the dog and back to the front door, turn to page 18.

If you make a dash for the kitchen, turn to page 21.

Brian and Jenny agree, and you all hop on your bikes and cruise down the street, keeping a sharp eye out for anything strange. When you get near Mr. Gravesend's house, you duck behind some bushes close to the street.

A single light burns in his house. The shades are pulled down, but you can see the outline of a person moving behind them. The figure is a good deal taller than Mr. Gravesend.

"That's not Gravesend," you say.

"Who could it be?" Jenny asks.

You don't answer her because at that moment a side door to the house opens. The figure you saw in the window steps out. It's a tall man wearing a dark jacket. You're pretty sure it's Eliot Sanger. He glances in your direction. The three of you freeze, hoping you won't be noticed in the shadows. He doesn't seem to see you and continues on across the street.

You all inch forward around the bushes and watch as he vaults over the four-foot-high wall in front of Sanger's house, clearing it by two or three feet.

Turn to page 82.

You reach up with your hand and feel blood trickling slowly down your neck. For some reason you want to taste it—it smells so good.

You lick your fingers and smack your lips. Then you turn and look at Eliot Sanger again. He is smiling at you, holding out his hand like an old and trusted friend.

The End

Your house is less than a block away. You hop on your bike and race home. No one is there, so you dial 911 and tell the dispatcher you think Maria is in trouble. He tells you to wait where you are.

A policeman named Officer Swartz arrives about three minutes later. You tell him the whole story.

He looks at you skeptically. "You haven't told me anything that makes me think a crime has been committed," he says.

"Yes, but I'm sure that the vampire lives in there," you say.

"We don't even know for sure that there *is* a vampire," he says. "There's no proof. As a matter of fact, there's no proof there even *are* vampires."

You start to argue, but he says, "Come on—we'll check into it."

Turn to page 25.

"Vampire?" He shakes his head. "Not a soul. No one but poor Mr. Sanger. Gone up in flames by now," he says, with a glance back toward the burning house.

The fireman heads off to where the chief is standing. You stand there awhile longer, watching the fire with your mom. It's beginning to die down, but by now there's not much left of the house.

Your mom nudges your arm. "Time to go home."

As the two of you walk back down the street, you think about the fire. Sanger must have known the police would raid the house. He set the fire so they wouldn't learn anything about him. He'll have to live someplace else now. But with his superhuman powers, that won't be hard.

Turn to page 68.

The next day after you get home from school, you receive a phone call from the detective.

"You were so helpful that I wanted to let you know what happened," he says. "We raided Mr. Sanger's house and Mr. Gravesend's house at the same time. Mr. Sanger's house was empty, but we found him at Mr. Gravesend's house. Lying in his coffin!"

"Wow. Did you arrest him?" you ask.

"We couldn't," the detective answers. "He died almost the moment he woke up. And then—and this is what's hardest of all to believe—he just shriveled up and disappeared."

"But he must have gone someplace!" you protest.

"I'm afraid that's true," he answers. "Every time a vampire dies, someone else becomes a vampire and takes his place."

"Is there any way of knowing who that will be?"

"It could be anybody," the detective answers. "It could be me. It could be you."

The End

"What would you do if you met one?" you ask.

Ms. Hallowell gives a little shudder. "I just hope I never do," she says. "The only sure way to deal with vampires is to stay away from them. People rarely survive when they are bitten by one. And if bitten, they may become vampires themselves!"

"Ick. How would I tell one if I saw him?" you ask.

Turn to page 20.

You and Brian head over to the vampire's house. At the last minute Jenny decides to come, too. When you get there, you all stand on tiptoe, craning your necks to look over the brick wall in front of the property.

The huge, dismal house, with its high-peaked gables and tall narrow windows, seems out of place in your neighborhood. Most of it is covered with vines. The lawn is overgrown. Crumbling stone steps lead to the front door, which looks as heavy as the door to a castle.

"What are you kids up to?" a voice calls from across the street. You all turn to see who is speaking. It's a frail-looking little man with thin white hair, a beaked nose, and glittering blue eyes.

"We think a vampire lives there," you say.

He limps a few steps closer to the curb. "How do you know *I'm* not the vampire?" he snaps back.

Startled, you back up a step, but then laugh. He's just trying to scare you. "You couldn't be," you say. "You'd have to be asleep in your coffin because it's daytime."

Turn to page 46.

You throw open the lid of the coffin. The sun streams in on you through the window. But it doesn't kill you. It feels good! You leap out of the coffin and onto the floor. You're in a room you've never seen before. Paintings of wilted flowers cover the walls. You're pretty sure you're still in Mr. Gravesend's house.

Now to get out of here! You run out of the room and down the hall. You notice that the next room is the one you were in before. Eliot's coffin is still there, though there is no sign of Mr. Gravesend.

You're not going to call out for him. Not after what he did to you! You take a last look at the coffin, wondering if Eliot really is in it and what would happen if you lifted the lid. Maybe he would die when the daylight hit him.

And the world would be rid of a dangerous vampire.

If he's not a vampire, it can't do any harm.

You're scared, but a powerful curiosity comes over you. You step over to the coffin. Bracing yourself to jump away, you try to lift the lid.

It's stuck.

Turn to page 75.

You break into a trot but suddenly stop short. You didn't realize it at the time, but you went through the woods at an angle. The house looming up ahead is Eliot Sanger's!

You shake off your fear and break into a run. *"Stop!"*

You see him in the shadows ahead. He's wearing the same black pants, white shirt, and cape he had on the night you first saw him.

Your only chance of escape would be to run back into the woods, but if you do that, he'll almost certainly track you down.

He begins moving slowly toward you, like a cat stalking its prey.

"Do not be afraid," he says in a soothing voice. "I have already feasted tonight. I don't need to taste any more blood for a week."

Turn to page 26.

40

"Don't hurt me!" you call out. "I promise never to tell anyone I met you!"

The vampire says nothing. He moves closer until he looms over you, dark and hulking. His eyes glint in the moonlight. He smiles and sniffs the air.

"You have warm, savory blood. A little salty—not too much—and slightly sweet."

"You promised you'd let me go!" you shriek.

He shakes out his cape. Leaning over you, he says, "You promised not to tell anyone you met me. But you cried out to the whole neighborhood!"

"I'm sorry—I didn't mean to. . . . Please let me go."

His lips curl up, exposing his white, curving fangs. He steps back, keeping his gaze on you. "All right. Go!" he cries.

Turn to page 55.

You start running and don't look back until you're halfway home. You go up to your room and sit on your bed, grateful to be safe, and almost surprised Sanger didn't attack you. Perhaps he had just drunk his evening meal and wasn't hungry. Whatever the explanation, you're determined never to go near Mr. Sanger's house again.

As you try to get to sleep that night, you can't stop thinking about Maria Murton. There was no sign of her in Sanger's house. She must have gotten out safely. At least you hope so. You'd better call her in the morning to make sure she got home all right.

Turn to page 22.

As soon as you stand up, you see what was attacking you: a bat, still hovering in front of the entrance to the cave, its tiny face wet with your blood.

You look around. The vampire is gone. You race past his house, climb over the wall in front of the property, and run down the street toward your home.

A car stops just ahead of you. There's a man in it. You're afraid it's the vampire! The door opens. The man leaps out. It's Mr. Conrad, Brian and Jenny's dad! Your friends are sitting in the backseat.

"I'm so glad we found you," Mr. Conrad says. "What happened? Your face is covered with blood. You look like you've been bitten by the vampire!"

Turn to page 80.

Mr. Gravesend leads you into the living room. The shades are drawn, but some light still gets through. A dark red rug covers the floor. There are two armchairs and a television set, which look normal enough. But where you might expect to find a sofa there's a shiny wooden coffin!

He stops before it and strokes the smooth, polished wood. "This is my stepson Eliot's," he says.

You step back a couple of paces toward the doorway. "Is Eliot sleeping in there?" you ask.

"Why wouldn't he be?" Mr. Gravesend says.

"You said vampires don't have to be in their coffins all day."

"You didn't hear me say that," he replies. "You just thought I said that."

This conversation is getting too spooky for you. "I think I'd better go now," you say.

Turn to page 8.

"Where?"

"It's gone now. It must have been the vampire!"

"What'll we do?" Brian cries. "It may break in!"

"There's one thing we've got that vampires are scared of," Jenny says. "Garlic! There's a bunch of it in the kitchen. If we crush it and rub it on ourselves, the vampire won't come near us!"

"How do you know that it will really work?" you ask nervously. "It may be just something people say."

"It's been proven for thousands of years," Jenny says firmly.

"Says who?" Brian mumbles. Suddenly you all jump—someone's banging on the front door. It sounds as if it's about to give way!

"Let's go out through the kitchen and run into the woods," Brian whispers. "We know our way around there, and the vampire doesn't. What do you think?"

If you say, "Let's try the garlic,"
turn to page 15.

If you say, "Let's head for the woods,"
turn to page 78.

"Now how do you know that?" he says. "That's what people *think*. You know who started that story?"

"Who?" Brian asks.

"The vampires themselves! That's one of their ways of fooling people."

"How do you know so much about vampires?" you ask.

He smiles. "I'll tell you," he says. "I'm Mr. Gravesend, by the way. My house is just across the street. Would you kids like some cider and cookies? I have some inside."

"Ah, no thanks," Brian says.

"Really? I'll tell you everything you need to know about vampires."

"Well, thanks, but we've got to be getting home," Jenny says. She gives you a little tap on the arm. "We'll talk later."

"Sure thing," you say, a little disappointed your friends are so chicken. You watch them bike off.

"Well," says the old man, "will *you* come in?" His glittering blue eyes twinkle at you.

If you accept his invitation, turn to page 19.

If you say, "No thanks," turn to page 53.

"What's your hurry?" a deep voice says from the shadows. A hand grips you from behind.

You start to scream, but the hand covers your face. You hear the voice behind you. "Don't make a sound and you'll be safe. I'm your new neighbor, Eliot Sanger. There's no reason we shouldn't be friends."

He lets you go. You shrink back and look into his face. He would be handsome if he weren't so deathly pale. He smiles, but it is a cruel smile, and his eyes burn into you like hot coals. By now you're certain he is a vampire.

"I—I'm sorry to be trespassing," you say. "I thought my friend came in here. I was looking for her."

"Oh. Well, I'm all alone here. Would you like to stay for dinner?" Sanger asks.

"No!" you almost shout. "I have to go home."

"Very well," he says. "I am sure we'll see each other again."

You hope not, but you don't want to argue with him. You keep silent until he has shown you safely out the door.

Turn to page 41.

You get out of bed and throw on some clothes. When you get downstairs, you find your mom has gotten dressed, too.

"Let's go see what's happening," she says, grabbing her coat. The two of you jog down the street. More fire engines roar by. You round the curve and see where they've stopped. Sanger's house is on fire! Bright orange flames leap up from the roof. A cloud of smoke is spreading over the neighborhood.

You and your mom join the crowd gathering behind the police lines. The firemen have a couple of hoses directed at the fire, but it's too late. The whole place is going up. You gasp as three firemen wearing masks and protective clothing come out of the front door and stagger away from the smoke and heat.

"Anyone who hasn't gotten out by now is a goner," a man near you says.

One of the three firemen passes you. He takes off his helmet and wipes his brow.

"Did you see anyone inside?" you ask. "Any sign of a vampire?"

Turn to page 34.

You're disappointed to hear this, and you're still worried about what has happened to Maria.

Officer Swartz lets you off outside your house. "Next time don't call 911 unless it's a real emergency," he warns.

"Sorry," you say. But you're not really sorry. You still think there *is* an emergency! For that reason you are not totally surprised when Officer Swartz comes to your door again the next day. This time a man in a suit is with him.

Turn to page 17.

50

You're tempted to continue on to the kitchen, and you start in that direction. You get about halfway there when the dog springs forward. It stands a few feet from you, a long, low growl coming from its throat.

You start back toward the dining room. Again the dog leaps ahead of you and blocks your way.

Turn to page 65.

52

You nod. "Down near the end of the block. Are you trying to find out if Sanger is a vampire?"

Maria slips her camera into her handbag. "Let's just say that I'm interested in him."

"Let's work together," you say.

"All right," she says after a moment. "You wait here. Don't follow me unless I signal you to."

"Okay." You stand and watch as she swings open the heavy iron gate and walks up to the front door of the house. She knocks. No one answers. She knocks again.

She waits a few minutes. Still no answer. She tries the door. It's unlocked. She opens it, peers inside, and walks in. Suddenly the door slams behind her! What's happening? You're tempted to run and see. But she said you should wait.

If you decide you'd better wait,
turn to page 9.

If you go up to the door and look in,
turn to page 11.

There's something about this man that makes you suspicious. You're sure he knows something about the vampire. "No, thanks," you tell him. "I'd rather not come in."

The next day, when you get home from school, your mom is waiting at the door.

"You missed a lot of excitement," she says. "A man was found dead in the park with all the blood drained out of him."

"That sounds like the work of a vampire," you say.

Your mom nods. "It does seem that way," she says gravely. "And whether the murderer is a vampire or not, we're going to have to be extra careful. Most important," she adds, pointing a finger at you, "I don't want you out after dark!"

Turn to page 77.

"You spilled my dinner!" booms a deep voice. You turn and see Sanger kick the dog aside and leap for you. With a swift motion, you bring the cauldron down over his head like an oversized hat!

"Lick the pot!" you scream at him as you turn and dive through the broken window. You hit the soft ground, breaking your fall with your hands. Then you're up and running as you've never run before.

You reach the brick wall at the front of the property and swing yourself over it.

"Stop!" The voice is not the vampire's. A police cruiser brakes alongside you, and an officer leans out the window. "What were you doing climbing over that wall? And what's that on your hands and shirt?"

Turn to page 83.

You take off toward the street, giving him a sidelong glance. In a few moments you reach the brick wall in front of his house. You climb over it, quick as a squirrel, and race down the street.

Your parents have locked the door, but they open it at once when they hear you knocking.

Your mom looks at you wide-eyed. "What happened? Why were you out at night?"

You start telling them about your adventures.

If you tell about your meeting with the vampire, turn to page 74.

If you keep your promise to the vampire and leave that part out, turn to page 81.

56

You awaken sometime later and immediately let out a scream. You're in a coffin! Thankfully, the lid is ajar. A little light comes through the crack. You start to push up on the lid, but then stop as a horrible thought comes into your mind. Suppose you've been changed into a vampire? If you push the lid open, you may die! Horrible as it seems, it might be safer to stay in the coffin until dark!

If you decide get out of the coffin right away, turn to page 38.

If you decide to stay in until dark, turn to page 62.

The next day Brian calls to tell you he and Jenny aren't allowed out past sunset. You decide to go back and investigate the Sanger house on your own that evening.

Again you watch Sanger leave Gravesend's house and walk across the street. Again he vaults over the wall, walks to the front door, turns a key in the latch, and goes inside.

This couldn't be a coincidence, you think. This man has to be a vampire, but instead of keeping his coffin in his own house, he keeps it across the street! That way if the police ever raid his house, they won't find him. Now you can tip off the police that if they raid Gravesend's house during daylight, they'll probably catch the vampire sleeping in his coffin!

You turn to head home and practically bump into Gravesend.

"What are you spying for?" he demands. "You'll come to a bad end, you will!" He reaches out for you, but you duck aside. You could easily outrun him—but you're tempted to stay around and see what you can learn from him.

If you stay and talk to him, turn to page 66.

If you take off for home, turn to page 28.

58

You, Brian, and Jenny have dinner in front of the TV and watch some game shows. Right in the middle of your favorite, the word WARNING flashes on the screen.

"Turn up the volume," Jenny says. "It's a special report."

Brian grabs the remote and clicks up the sound.

"Police say they are working round-the-clock to find the vampire," the newscaster says. "In the last few hours they have developed some promising new leads. We can only hope that they'll pay off before the vampire strikes again. Meanwhile, everyone should be extra cautious. And don't go out at night alone!"

The news switches back to the game show, and Brian turns the set off.

"Hey, you know—" you start to say, when Jenny taps your shoulder.

"Shhh."

You hear the wind outside, rustling the leaves. Then a creaking sound.

Turn to page 61.

You realize that if you went to call the police, the sun could set before they got here. You run up to the house and cautiously open the door.

The house is dark and very quiet. You step into the hallway far enough so you can look into the living room. Heavy drapes cover the windows. Two or three large wooden chairs are pulled in front of a great stone fireplace. The only light comes from a dim table lamp.

Your eyes are drawn to the far wall. On it is a large portrait of a man with dark, slick hair, pure white skin, and deep red lips. His eyes burn with an unnatural light. You can't stop looking at the painting until you hear chimes—the hall clock striking 6:00 P.M. The sun has probably set by now. You've *got* to get out of here!

Turn to page 47.

60

After talking to Ms. Hallowell, you hop on your bike and head for Sanger's house. There's no sign of Brian. You lean your bike up against the four-foot-high brick wall in front of the property and peer over at the house.

It's almost a mansion, with four sharp-pointed gables and tall, thick chimneys at either end.

A car pulls up a little way down the street. A woman with brown hair and a long tan coat gets out and walks toward you. You watch as she takes out a camera and snaps several pictures of the house. She makes a note on a pad she's holding.

"What are you doing?" you ask her.

Turn to page 69.

"That's the gate swinging in the wind," Brian says. "I guess someone didn't close it tightly."

"Someone should go out and close it," Jenny says.

"Not me," says Brian.

They both look at you. You shake your head.

"Yiiiikes!" Jenny shrieks.

"What?"

"I saw a face in the window!"

Turn to page 45.

You decide to stay in the coffin. If you've become a vampire, it's the only safe place for you until sunset.

With nothing to do but lie there for the rest of the afternoon, you close your eyes and rest, trying not to think about vampires. After a while you fall asleep. And you dream. You dream that you feel bite marks on your neck. Then you're drinking water, then milk, then orange juice, and then . . . *blood!*

Suddenly you're awakened by people calling your name. Someone is shaking you.

The lid of the coffin is wide open. It's late afternoon, but the sun is pouring in the window, striking your face. It's not hurting you a bit!

"I'm alive!" you cry. Only then do you notice the people standing over you—your mother and Mr. Gravesend.

"Of course you're alive," your mom says. "And you've got a lot of explaining to do."

You jump out of the coffin, happy to be standing on the floor again.

"How did you find me?" you ask your mom.

Turn to page 10.

"Come along," he says. "We're only going into the family room. There's nothing to be afraid of."

You stop a moment, considering whether to follow him. On the one hand, you don't really trust him. On the other hand, he's so small and frail that you're sure you could get away if he tried to hurt you. You follow him through a hallway, taking care to keep a few steps behind him.

This part of the house is much darker. Pictures of dead and drooping flowers line the walls—just what you might expect to see in a vampire's house! Maybe vampires don't have to be in their coffins all day. Maybe Mr. Gravesend is a vampire himself!

Turn to page 44.

You test the dog several times more, but it will only let you move a few inches either way before it plants itself in front of you, teeth bared, a low growl lingering in its throat.

You stand there helplessly. At some point the dog will leave. It can't stay there forever any more than you can.

The afternoon wears on. You wonder what happened to Maria. You haven't heard any sounds from elsewhere in the house. She must have left, not knowing you were trapped here.

You keep watching the dog out of the corner of your eye, hoping it will go away. After a while, it lies down between you and the dining room. But its eyes never leave you.

Turn to page 29.

"I wasn't spying. Why are you so worried?" you ask the old man.

"That's my business," he replies. "And your business better be to stay home and stop prying into things!"

"Well, you're prying into *my* business!" you snap back. "This is a free country. I have a right to stand here."

Gravesend doesn't seem to know what to say next. He gives you a strange smile.

"What are you smiling at?" you demand. A second later you find out, as sharp fangs pierce your neck! You break free, wheel around, and look up at the cruel, ghastly face of Eliot Sanger. His image blurs. You sway dizzily.

Moments later your vision returns. Even in the dim light, everything you look at seems sharp and clear. You hear a cat mewing far away, then voices coming from the house next door.

Turn to page 32.

"It looks like the vampire is still loose," you tell your mom. "He must be sleeping in a coffin somewhere at this very moment."

"I'm afraid so," she says. "And tonight he'll be out again, looking for his next victim."

You nod grimly. You have a feeling it's going to be you!

The End

She smiles at you. "Why do you want to know?"

"Because I'm curious about the man who lives there."

"His name is Mr. Sanger," she says.

"Yes, I know that. But I want to find out what he's like."

"Well," she says, "I'm here for the same reason. My name is Maria Murton. I'm a reporter for the *Daily Times*."

"Hi," you say. "You're a friend of the Conrads, aren't you?"

"That's right," says Maria, giving you a grin. "Do you live in the neighborhood?"

Turn to page 52.

70

"Hey! It's us! Were you afraid to come to the door?" a man calls out.

"We forgot our keys!" a woman says. In a moment they are both standing in the kitchen doorway. It's Mr. and Mrs. Conrad!

Jenny runs up to hug them. "Are we glad it's you! We thought it was the vampire!"

"Wow, you kids stink!" her dad exclaims. "What is that—garlic?"

"It was to fend off the vampire," you explain.

"Well, I guess it worked," Mrs. Conrad says. "I don't see any around here!"

The End

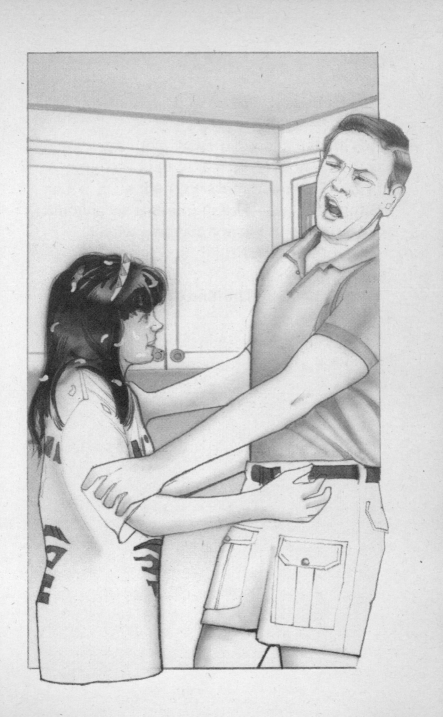

"It's been sold. The man who owned it has left town."

"Well, that's good news," you say. "Who bought the house?"

"I don't know," she says. "It's such a big, gloomy old place—I can't imagine who would want to live in it. Except maybe a witch."

Or another vampire.

The End

It doesn't. The only way out would be through one of the small windows over the kitchen counter, and they're latched shut.

Your eyes fasten on a cauldron on the stove. Simmering inside is a dark red liquid. It must be some kind of soup, but the smell of it makes you sick to your stomach. Suddenly you realize it's not soup. It's blood!

The whistle sounds again. The door from the pantry swings open. The dog is back, coming at you, its jaws open and ready to clamp your neck!

It takes all your strength, but you grab a dishtowel to protect your hands, lift the cauldron from the stove, and hurl its contents at the dog. He lets out a yelp and leaps back, hot blood dripping from his head and body.

You drop the cauldron on the counter, then climb up and try to unlatch the windows. They won't budge. You swing the cauldron against one and break it, then knock out the shards of broken glass.

Turn to page 54.

As soon as you've caught your breath, you tell your parents everything that happened. They listen, astonished, especially when you tell them about the vampire. Just as you finish, the phone rings. Your dad answers it and talks for a few minutes.

"That was Mrs. Conrad," he tells you and your mom after he hangs up. "She called to see if you had come home. She said that when she and Mr. Conrad arrived back from dinner, they found that Jenny, Brian, and you were all missing. They called the police. By the time the cops came, Brian and Jenny had returned from the woods where they were hiding."

Your mom gives a little shudder. "I sure hope they catch him," she says.

You sleep fitfully that night. You keep having nightmares where the vampire comes to get you. Finally you drift into a deep sleep.

At dawn you are awakened by fire engines. They sound as if they're stopping near the other end of the street. You rush to the window. There's light in the east, where the sun will be rising. And from the opposite direction, down the street, comes a red, flickering glow.

Turn to page 48.

You check to see if the lid of the coffin is nailed down or if there's a lock. You don't see one. You squat down like a weight lifter and press up hard.

The lid suddenly pops up.

"Oh!" you shriek, jumping back. The vampire *is* lying there, his dark, oily hair combed neatly over his ears, his eyes shut. Except for his scarlet lips, his face is as white as a ghost's.

He lets out a gasp, revealing his long, curved fangs. The sight of him is horrible, but for some reason you can't turn away.

From deep within his throat comes a great wail, like the howl of a lone wolf. He sits up and points a long, arched finger at you. Then, flinging out his arms, he collapses and begins to shrivel up, blackening and smoking like bacon left on a hot flame!

You stand there, frozen in horror. Finally you get hold of yourself and turn to run.

Only your way is blocked.

Mr. Gravesend is standing in the doorway, a thick wooden cane in his hand. He looks at you with hatred in his eyes.

Turn to page 13.

He let out a cackling laugh. "A clever answer. Well, first of all I know that my stepson is a vampire."

"What? That's horrible!"

He gives you a peculiar smile. 'I know. It *is* horrible. But do you think I get any sympathy? No. People hate me, as if it were my fault!" He pushes the cookie plate closer to you even though it's already within easy reach.

"You've got to be kidding about your son being a vampire," you say.

"You think so?" he snaps back. "Come with me." He gets up and motions for you to follow.

By now you don't know what to make of him. You're thinking that maybe you should get out of there. Besides, you're beginning to feel a little funny.

Turn to page 64.

That night Brian and Jenny come over to your house for an early supper.

"I don't think they're ever going to catch the vampire," Brian says as he finishes his dessert.

"He may end up drinking the blood of everyone in this town," Jenny says.

"Then he'll move on to the next town," says Brian.

"Well, maybe we better catch him ourselves," you say.

"You've got to be kidding," Brian says. "How would we do that?"

"That man we met—Mr. Gravesend. I think he has some connection with the vampire," you say. "You saw how weird he seemed."

"That doesn't mean much. There are weirdos everywhere," Jenny says.

"Suppose he *is* connected with him," Brian says. "What would we do about it?"

You glance out the window. The sun has set, but there's still plenty of light in the sky. "Let's bike past his place," you say. "Maybe we'll learn something."

Turn to page 30.

"Let's head for the woods," you say.

"Everyone follow me!" Brian says. He tears through the dining room into the kitchen and unlatches the kitchen door. He opens it a crack and looks out. Loud pounding continues on the front door.

"Hurry," Brian says in a hoarse whisper. "Keep as quiet as possible and follow me." He runs out into the darkness.

Jenny follows, with you last. "Close the door tight!" she calls back to you.

You try to shut the door, but it won't stay shut. Finally you get it to stay and run to catch up with the twins. In the darkness you can't see where they went. There's only dense undergrowth at the beginning of the woods.

You grope around, trying to find your way through the brush. You don't dare yell out for your friends—the vampire would hear you for sure.

By now your eyes are getting used to the dark. You look back and see a tall figure coming around the side of the house. It must be the vampire, going to try the back door!

Turn to page 7.

You turn and run for the cave, with the vampire on your heels! It's almost pitch-black—one stumble and you'll be flat on your face. But you keep your footing and dive into the cave, inches ahead of his grasping hand.

You crawl farther into the cave. It's hardly bigger around than you are, but it seems quite deep. A second later you feel a jab at your feet. The vampire is reaching in with a stick! You hear his cape rip as it tears on the sharp rock at the entrance. He lets out an angry curse.

You wiggle in farther still, brushing the roof with your shoulders. Dirt falls on you, sifting past your ears and down your cheeks.

Suddenly something flies at you. Tiny, sharp teeth dig into your forehead, biting for blood.

"Ahhh!" you scream, throwing a hand up to protect yourself. You wiggle backward, but the creature is still flying at your face, biting your ear, then your cheek and neck. You can't worry about the vampire now—you back out of the cave as fast as you can!

Turn to page 42.

80

"A vampire bat!" you wail.

You hope that's all it was. Already you're feeling strangely giddy. Newfound strength is flowing into your limbs. Though it is late in the evening, everything you look at is sharp and clear, as if it were the middle of the day. At the same time you're feeling extremely thirsty. And you have a new, strange craving—for blood!

The End

You want to tell everyone what happened, but you don't dare. You know that vampires have superhuman powers. If you don't keep your promise, you're afraid he'll somehow find out.

From then on, you hardly talk to anyone about Sanger, and you stay clear of his house. Nothing happens to you, but every once in a while you hear that another person in your town is missing. You keep hoping the police will catch Sanger, and that it will be proved that he's the vampire. But weeks go by without any news of him.

One day, when you've almost begun to forget about him, you come home from school and find your mom talking on the phone.

"Guess what?" she tells you when she hangs up. "That big old house down the road—the one people thought might be owned by the vampire . . ."

"What about it?" you ask eagerly.

Turn to page 72.

"Wow! That's no ordinary man," Jenny says.

The three of you stare as he turns a key in the latch and lets himself in.

"So now we know!" you exclaim. "Eliot Sanger is the vampire. He sleeps during the daytime in Mr. Gravesend's house."

"We can't be sure he's a vampire," Brian says. "It may have been just a coincidence that he left Mr. Gravesend's house just after sunset. He may be just an ordinary man who visits there for some reason."

"I'm sure he's the vampire," you say.

"I'm not," Brian says. "Let's come back at the same time tomorrow. See if he does it again."

"Sounds good to me," you say. "It's getting pretty dark. I've got to get home."

"So do we," Jenny says.

Suddenly you see the door open. "Shhh," you whisper, pointing. "He's coming out of the house again."

Turn to page 16.

You realize that you're dripping with the blood that spilled out of the cauldron.

"Is that blood on you?" the officer asks, getting out of his car. "Are you hurt?"

"No, I'm okay."

By now he is standing beside you. Darkness has settled. He shines a flashlight on your face, chest, and arms. "You don't have any cuts at all!" he says indignantly.

"No, I don't," you say. "I'll explain everything."

"You'd better," he says. "Or I'll have to report that I have a young vampire on my hands."

The End

The two policemen look at each other. "We shouldn't tell you," Paterno says.

"Tell me!" you insist. "I've got to know!"

Paterno brushes his hand across his face. "All right," he says in a grave voice. "There were dried-up bodies lying there, every drop of blood drained out of them."

"So, Eliot Sanger *is* a vampire," you murmur.

"Yes, there's not much doubt of that now," Paterno says. "At least he knows he can't come back to his house."

But where will he show up next?

The End

Sanger's piercing eyes fix on you. When he smiles, his dark lips part, revealing long, gleaming fangs.

"No," you whisper, your heart racing as he reaches for you. You fall back and scream.

And he screams, too! The woman's dog has seized him by the ankle!

In that instant you wheel away and race across the street. Looking back over your shoulder, you see Sanger vault across a fence.

The dog bounds back to his mistress, wagging his tail.

"Good boy, Dusty!" the woman says, patting him. "Yes, you're a very good boy."

"Excuse me, ma'am," you call to her. "Do you know where I can get a dog like that?"

The End

TILL YOU

With each and every one of these scary, creepy, delightfully, frightfully funny books, you'll be dying to go to the *Graveyard School!*

Order any or all of the books in this scary new series by **Tom B. Stone**! Just check off the titles you want, then fill out and mail the order form below.

☐	0-553-48223-8	**DON'T EAT THE MYSTERY MEAT!**	$3.50/$4.50 Can.
☐	0-553-48224-6	**THE SKELETON ON THE SKATEBOARD**	$3.50/$4.50 Can.
☐	0-553-48225-4	**THE HEADLESS BICYCLE RIDER**	$3.50/$4.50 Can.
☐	0-553-48226-2	**LITTLE PET WEREWOLF**	$3.50/$4.50 Can.
☐	0-553-48227-0	**REVENGE OF THE DINOSAURS**	$3.50/$4.50 Can.